The *New* Goldilocks and the Three Bears

Mama Bear, Mommy Bear & Baby Bear

written and illustrated by Beth McMurray

Copyright © 2012 by Beth McMurray. All rights reserved. No part of this publication may be reproduced, stored in any retrieval system or transmitted, in any form or by any means, without the prior written permission of the publisher. For information regarding permission, write to: inksproutpress@gmail.com. Published by Ink Sprout Press. ISBN: 978-1479389285

Once upon a time, there was a happy family of three teddy bears—Mama Bear, Mommy Bear, and Baby Bear. They lived together in a cozy house in the woods.

One afternoon, Baby Bear helped Mama Bear make fresh lemonade while Mommy Bear cooked a hearty soup.

Mommy Bear stirred the steaming pot of soup. "Want to go for a walk while the soup cools?"

"Great idea," said Mama Bear. "I'll set out the bowls so we can pour the soup before we leave."

The three bears left their steaming bowls of soup on the kitchen table and set off for a walk.

While the three bears were walking, a young girl was hiking through the woods. Her name was Goldilocks, and her shining yellow hair matched her name.

Goldilocks hiked further than usual that day. She had finished all her water, but was still very thirsty. She became tired and weak without water.

She was about to turn around when she spotted a house. She wasn't sure she could make the long walk home without having something more to drink.

She went to the door and knocked, almost collapsing from fatigue. There was no answer because the house belonged to the three bears who were out on a walk.

Goldilocks peeked in the window to see if anyone was home. She didn't see anyone. Through the window, though, she saw three pitchers of lemonade. The lemonade looked cool and refreshing, and she was very thirsty. She knocked again, but there was still no answer. Out of desperation she tried the door and, sure enough, it opened! Goldilocks was relieved. She could get something to drink at last!

Goldilocks rushed over to the first pitcher of lemonade, which belonged to Mama Bear. She poured a glass, and took a sip. "Yuck!" Goldilocks said. "This lemonade is too sour!"

She tried the next pitcher of lemonade, which belonged to Mommy Bear. She poured a glass, and took a sip. "Yuck!" Goldilocks said. "This lemonade is too sweet!"

She grabbed the third pitcher of lemonade, which belonged to Baby Bear. She poured a glass, and took a sip. "Ah, just right!" Goldilocks said. "Not too sweet and not too sour."

The lemonade was so tasty and refreshing that she drank the entire glass in a few quick gulps. She refilled the glass again and again until the entire pitcher of lemonade was empty.

Just as Goldilocks finished the last sip of lemonade, a loud growl echoed in the kitchen. "What was that?" she asked quietly. The loud growl roared again. "Oh," said Goldilocks. "Silly me. That's my stomach." Goldilocks had been hiking so long she had missed lunch. Her stomach growled again, and she realized she should eat before she started on the long walk home. She had been so thirsty, she had forgotten how hungry she was!

Goldilocks saw three bowls of soup cooling on the kitchen table. The soup smelled delicious! Goldilocks grabbed the spoon from the first bowl, which belonged to Mama Bear. She took a taste. "Yuck!" Goldilocks said. "This soup is too salty!"

She grabbed the spoon from the second bowl, which belonged to Mommy Bear. She took a taste. "Yuck!" Goldilocks said. "This soup is too bland."

She grabbed the spoon from the third bowl, which belonged to Baby Bear. She took a taste. "Ah, just right!" Goldilocks said. "Not too salty and not too bland." The soup was so tasty that she ate the entire bowl.

After drinking an entire pitcher of lemonade and eating a big bowl of soup, Goldilocks was tired. She decided she should rest before she started on the long walk home.

She went into the living room and sat in Mama Bear's chair. "Ack!" Goldilocks said. "This chair is too hard!"

She got up and sat in Mommy Bear's chair. "Ack!" Goldilocks said. "This chair is too soft!"

She got up and sat in Baby Bear's chair. "Ah, just right!" Goldilocks said. "Not too hard and not too soft." She sat in Baby Bear's chair until she grew sleepy.

Goldilocks decided she should take a short nap before she started on the long walk home. She went upstairs and found three beds.

She crawled into Mama Bear's bed. "Ack!" Goldilocks said. "This blanket is too heavy!"

She crawled into Mommy Bear's bed. "Ack!" Goldilocks said. "This blanket is too light!"

She crawled into Baby Bear's bed. "Ah, just right!" Goldilocks said. "Not too heavy and not too light." She quickly fell asleep in Baby Bear's bed and dreamed about all the pretty flowers in the woods.

Meanwhile, the three bears were returning home. When they got to the front door, Mama Bear looked puzzled. "The door is open!"

"That's odd," Mommy Bear said. "I'm sure we closed it before our walk."

The three bears went inside. Right away they noticed things were out of place. "Somebody has been drinking my lemonade!" Mama Bear said.

"Somebody has been drinking my lemonade, too!" Mommy Bear said.

"Somebody drank my lemonade, too," Baby Bear said. "And they drank it all!"

As Mama Bear tried to comfort Baby Bear, Mommy Bear noticed the spoon in her soup had been moved. "Somebody has been eating my soup!" Mommy Bear said.

Mama Bear rushed over. "Somebody has been eating my soup, too!" Mama Bear said.

"Somebody ate my soup, too," Baby Bear said. "And they ate it all!"

Baby Bear was sad and walked into the living room. Mama Bear and Mommy Bear followed Baby Bear into the living room.

"Somebody has been sitting in my chair!" Mama Bear said.

"Somebody has been sitting in my chair, too!" Mommy Bear said.

"Somebody has been sitting in my chair, too!" Baby Bear said.

"We better check upstairs," said Mama Bear.

The three bears went upstairs. Right away, Mama Bear noticed the blanket on her bed was ruffled. "Somebody has been lying in my bed!" Mama Bear said.

"Somebody has been lying in my bed, too!" Mommy Bear said.

"Somebody is SLEEPING in my bed!" Baby Bear yelled.

Upon hearing Baby Bear yell, Goldilocks woke up with a start. She saw the three bears and jumped out of bed in fear. Images of sharp claws and pointy teeth raced through her head. Goldilocks didn't realize these were three cuddly teddy bears who meant no harm. She ran to the window and jumped out.

Luckily for Goldilocks, a big, leafy lemon tree grew right under the window and cushioned her fall. She came away with only some small scratches.

As she plucked a leaf out of her hair, a lemon bopped her on the head. That bop on the head jolted her out of her fright. She looked at the bright yellow lemon and remembered the tasty lemonade that had quenched her thirst.

"Those bears had tasty lemonade and I drank an entire pitcher," Goldilocks said to herself. "And I ate an entire bowl of soup. I sat in their chairs, messed up their beds, and even took a nap in their house!"

Goldilocks had an idea. She collected the lemons on the ground under the lemon tree. With a handful of lemons, she went to the front door of the house and knocked. Mama Bear opened the door.

"I'm sorry I disrupted your house," Goldilocks said. "Maybe I can help make more lemonade since I drank an entire pitcher." Goldilocks offered the lemons to the three bears.

The bears accepted the lemons and invited Goldilocks in to make lemonade. All three bears and Goldilocks helped squeeze the lemons to make juice.

When all the lemons were squeezed, Baby Bear grabbed the sugar.

"I like just the right amount of sugar," Baby Bear said. "So it's not too sweet and not too sour."

"I agree!" said Goldilocks.

And it turned out that Goldilocks and Baby Bear agreed on a lot more than just lemonade. They had many things in common and became good friends. Goldilocks came over to play at Baby Bear's house often—but she always called first to make sure the three bears were home!

34105363R00018

Made in the USA
Middletown, DE
08 August 2016